THE X

Regene[illegible]ion

Other X-Files books in this series

The Calusari

Eve

Bad Sign

Our Town

Empathy

Fresh Bones

Control

The Host

Hungry Ghosts

Dark Matter

Howlers

Grotesque

Quarantine

Haunted

THE X FILES™

Regeneration

Novelization by Everett Owens

Based on the television series
The X-Files created by
Chris Carter

Based on the teleplay
written by Vince Gilligan, John Shiban,
and Frank Spotnitz

HarperCollins*Entertainment*
An Imprint of HarperCollins*Publishers*

HarperCollins*Entertainment*
An Imprint of HarperCollins*Publishers*
77–85 Fulham Palace Road,
Hammersmith, London W6 8JB

www.**fireandwater**.com

This paperback edition 2000
1 3 5 7 9 8 6 4 2

First published in the USA by HarperEntertainment
A division of HarperCollins Publishers Inc.

A catalogue record for this book
is available from the British Library

ISBN 0 00 658353 4

Set in Goudy

Printed and bound in Great Britain by
Caledonian International Book Manufacturing Ltd, Glasgow

Chapter One

The Pittsburgh city hospital ambulance crested a hill, its pulsing lights and shrill siren cutting through the night sky. The EMT behind the wheel, Michele Wilkes, maneuvered the ambulance through the traffic, swerving left then right. Despite the noise and action around her, Wilkes's eyes never left the road—a discipline her years on the job had made instinctive. This late on a Friday night, she knew she had to be especially careful. Wilkes pulled her radio microphone off its rack and switched it on.

"We're en route with a male cardiac, age sixty-two. Estimated time of arrival, twelve minutes," she said, keeping the message short.

The dispatcher responded in kind.

"Copy, ETA in twelve. Crash unit standing by."

Wilkes allowed herself a glance in the rearview mirror.

"How's he looking, Leonard?"

Wilkes's senior partner, Leonard Betts, was hunched over an elderly black man in the back of the ambulance, simultaneously checking his heartbeat with a stethoscope and a digital heart monitor.

"He's up to his ass in alligators," Betts answered calmly.

Just as he spoke, the monitor emitted a series of short, piercing beeps. The patient gasped loudly, then began gulping for air. Wilkes could hear the monitor going crazy.

"Is he going into arrest?" she shouted.

Ignoring the question, Betts pulled off the stethoscope and put his ear to the man's chest. Satisfied with what he heard, Betts called back to Wilkes. "No, he's not."

Betts reached back into a drawer and pulled out a large hypodermic syringe. Shucking its plastic sleeve and removing the safety tip, Betts jabbed it into the man's windpipe. Instantly, air whistled out through the barrel, and the monitor resumed a steady rhythm. The patient's breathing returned to normal.

Wilkes heard the monitor's calm beeping from the cab and wondered what had just happened.

"What'd you do?" she asked her partner.

Moving efficiently, Betts taped down the syringe. He remained vigilant as he briefed Wilkes.

"Aspirated his chest," he explained. "He has a tension pneumothorax pressing on his heart. It just looked like a cardiac."

Wilkes shook her head, quietly impressed. It never ceased to amaze her that, no matter how dire the situation, Leonard sounded like he was treating a stubbed toe.

"Nice catch," she said, keeping her eyes on the road. "How did you know?"

Betts stared hard at his unconscious patient, looking the man over as if he could almost see through the skin. Finally, he murmured, "Because he's dying of cancer. It's eaten through one lung already."

Wilkes was keenly aware of the equipment available to EMTs in an ambulance. There was no way Leonard could tell this at this point.

"How do you know, Leonard?" she shook her head in wonder.

But Betts didn't answer. He continued to stare into the man's chest. Wilkes turned her head to look back at him for a moment. She wanted to know how he did it, how he always knew ahead of time what doctors at the hospital would confirm hours later. With her head turned, she didn't notice the stoplight ahead of her change from green to red.

The sound of a car horn caused Wilkes to whip her head around. The tow truck's headlights caught the side of her face an instant before the vehicle plowed into her. The violence of the crash shattered metal and flesh like a bomb blast. The ambulance, which had been cruising north, was slammed sideways by the truck, sending it sliding in a shower of broken glass before it crashed into a streetlamp that buckled halfway up. The top section of the streetlamp teetered, then fell down onto the wreckage, illuminating the cab of the tow truck where the driver lay slumped over the wheel, his horn still blaring.

Dazed but conscious, Wilkes pushed the ambulance door open and stumbled out. Blood dripped onto her uniform from a wound on her forehead. She steadied herself by holding on to the mangled door of the ambulance.

"Leonard?" she called out, but there was no answer. Other than the tow truck's horn, the deserted downtown street was quiet as a tomb.

Wilkes picked her way to the back of the ambulance and found the back doors hanging wide open. Nervously, she looked inside, where she discovered the patient lying dead, strapped to a blood-spattered gurney that had flipped over on its side. The heart monitor showed a blue flatline shimmering across its screen. All the medical equipment—the bandages, bottles, pumps, IV bags—had been thrown around the compartment by the impact. But Wilkes still didn't see her partner.

"Leonard!" she yelled.

She turned from the wreckage and scanned the scene. Eventually her eyes fell on a pair of legs stretched out along the sidewalk thirty or forty feet away. A row of newspaper racks concealed the body from the waist up. Wilkes staggered toward the limbs, ducking underneath a utility pole cable, and making her way around the racks. As she did, the rest of the body came into view.

Most of it, anyway.

A wave of nausea hit Wilkes, and she had to cover her mouth to keep from vomiting. She stumbled, then braced herself against one of the newspaper racks and forced herself to look again. Leonard Betts's blue-and-white uniformed body sprawled before her, lying stomach-down in a pool of blood that spurted from the stump of his neck.

"Oh, God. Leonard!" Wilkes cried, her body shuddering helplessly.

Then she saw it, just a few feet away, lodged between a car tire and the curb. Leonard Betts's eyes, frozen open, stared back at her from his severed head.

Michele Wilkes stood in the doorway of the Monongahela Medical Center morgue. She watched as a night attendant lifted a sheet from the body of the patient she was supposed to deliver to the emergency ward five hours earlier. Now, instead of resting in a recovery room, the man lay on the stainless-steel drawer of a morgue freezer. The attendant swiftly slid the corpse into the compartment and slammed the door shut, the latch clicking shut with what struck Wilkes as appropriate finality.

Wilkes had come down to the morgue to say goodbye to Leonard, the best partner an EMT could hope for—always calm, always helpful, always dead-on in his diagnoses. Leonard may have been a loner—the two of them had never done anything socially together—but she'd always liked him and considered herself lucky to be his partner. Wilkes couldn't decide whether she was relieved or disappointed that his body had already been prepped and put away by the time she arrived. She watched the morgue attendant label two tags and slide them into their tiny frames beneath the handles of the drawers. Then she waited until the attendant disappeared into an adjoining office before entering. She knew she was probably making him uneasy, but this was something she needed to do.

Wilkes crossed the gleaming white tile floor to a row of drawers holding the recently deceased. There, in felt tip, read the name BETTS, LEONARD M. She pressed her fingertips to the stainless steel drawer and whispered, "I'm sorry, Leonard. I am so sorry."

Greg Jones was a first-year medical student. And unlike some of his friends, he took his training seriously—very seriously. Maybe that was why he was the only first-year student willing to take the most morbid work-study job: morgue attendant.

He didn't mind it. Most of the time, he was able to get a lot done while on duty. And here in the morgue office, more than any place, he was able to study undisturbed. The silence, however, sometimes got to him. That's why he brought his Walkman to work. Flipping a page in his text, Jones began to highlight a chapter heading when he heard something unusual above the music, a faint metallic rattling. He turned down the music and listened more attentively.

A thump.

He clicked off the Walkman and removed the earphones. Jones sat bolt upright.

"Hello?" he shouted into the dimness of the morgue.

A crash from the lab made Jones jump out of his seat. Shaking, he took a deep breath before calling out again, "Hello? Is someone there?" When there was no answer, he ventured a few steps, turning cautiously into the main room. He stopped short when he saw one of the freezer drawers open and empty. It was too dark to read the tag, but he could remember the name; he had written out the tag only an hour earlier—Betts, Leonard M. Crossing farther into the room, Jones passed a table. Below it, on the floor beneath the freezer, was a volleyball-sized lump under a white sheet.

Jones glanced around him before hunkering down

to lift the sheet. Underneath was the bruised and nearly frozen head of Leonard Betts.

As Jones lowered the sheet, he sensed someone approaching. He turned, but he wasn't fast enough. He saw a shiny steel bar—a morgue tool used to break bones—raised above him. It came down, and Jones crumpled to the ground. The last thing he saw before plunging into unconsciousness was the distorted figure of a man reflected in the stainless steel of the morgue drawers. Though the reflection was cloudy, one thing was perfectly clear—the figure had no head.

Chapter Two

The forensic technician bent low to the morgue floor, pointed his camera at the bloody sheet, and snapped a number of photographs from slightly varying angles. The head that had been concealed by the sheet the night before was no longer there.

Special Agent Dana Scully was surveying the morgue, wondering why she had been called by her partner so early in the morning. Scully swung the square silver door open and peeked into the empty freezer. Using her penlight, she illuminated the darkest recesses of the drawer, taking note of the blood that pooled in the spot where a head might typically rest. Scully had opened more morgue drawers than she cared to remember, but this was the first time that she consciously took note of the dimensions. The compartment was deep—seven feet, she guessed—but it had no more than eighteen inches of vertical clearance. No room for maneuvering—not that the dead required much space. The footprints on the inside face of the drawer's door, however, struck her as exceedingly strange. One of the forensic technicians had discovered them by dusting the inside of the door with a red powder. As unlikely as that was, it looked as if the door to the compartment had been kicked out from the inside.

Scully's partner, Special Agent Fox Mulder, stepped in beside her and peered into the recess.

"Cozy," he said, jokingly. "Who'd want to leave?"

"I guess whoever happened to get locked in here last night," Scully replied.

Mulder opened the case file he was carrying.

"Well, that would be Leonard Morris Betts, age thirty-four. But it should probably be noted that when Mr. Betts arrived last night, he was sans head."

Mulder referred back to his notes.

"Decapitated when his ambulance crashed. He was an emergency medical technician for this hospital. A highly regarded one, apparently: a slew of commendations, and write-ups in the local paper."

Scully listened, not sure what any of it meant and not finding it particularly intriguing.

"What about the morgue attendant on duty at the time?" she asked.

Mulder checked the notes again.

"Somebody coldcocked him and stole his clothes. He didn't see who. No alarms were tripped, so no one broke in."

Scully nodded, waiting, but Mulder had nothing more to say. She shrugged. "And?"

"Weird, huh?"

Scully considered the facts, but the truth was, she didn't find it all that weird.

"Mulder," she asked, "what the hell are we doing here?"

He smiled.

"Did I mention Mr. Betts had no head?"

"Yes, you did," Scully retorted. "And I hope you're not suggesting a headless body kicked its way out of a latched morgue freezer."

Mulder shrugged innocently.

"Are you?" Scully asked, furrowing her brows. "Because this is obviously just a bizarre attempt at a cover-up."

"Meant to conceal what?" Mulder asked flatly.

"My guess would be body snatching for profit. There's a shortage of teaching cadavers at medical schools."

Mulder nodded as if he had already considered this, but Scully finished her thought.

"An unscrupulous medical supplier might pay top dollar. No questions asked."

"Then why take a headless man and leave so many complete bodies behind?" Mulder asked.

Before Scully could answer, a young uniformed police officer approached Mulder.

"Sir?" he asked, not wanting to interrupt the two federal agents. Mulder turned to him. "Those video grabs you asked for? I think we found something."

Mulder and Scully followed the cop, who walked briskly past the stacked rows of freezer drawers to one of the examination tables and laid out six eight-by-ten black-and-white photos. The grainy shots showed a man, from the back only, slouching through the deserted hospital and exiting into the night.

"These are from the emergency-room camera, taken at four-thirteen this morning," the cop explained.

Scully pointed to the clearest of the photos.

"There's your perp," she told Mulder, "wearing the stolen uniform."

Mulder picked up the photo from the table and held it closer to his eyes.

"Looks like it," he said, "though there's not much else to be learned from these, unfortunately."

There was something strange about the photos that was bothering Mulder. In each one, a faint fog or lens flare obscured the man—especially his head—from view. The fogging showed up only on the man, nowhere else in the photos, and his location within the photograph didn't seem to make any difference.

Mulder pointed it out to the cop.

"What are these flares?"

The cop leaned in closer.

"Bad video," he replied. "The security system isn't exactly state-of-the-art."

Mulder nodded to the cop, but Scully recognized this gesture. It meant, "You're wrong, but I'm not going to waste my time arguing with you." Suddenly, Mulder had a new point that had nothing to do with the blurred photographs.

"If this is our guy, what did he do with the corpse he stole? He's not carrying anything."

"Maybe he got spooked and was forced to abandon it," Scully suggested.

"They've combed the facility completely, Scully. Where could he hide an adult body where it couldn't be found?"

Scully pondered the question for a moment, then realized it was an easy riddle for someone who'd spent as much time as she had around dead bodies.

"I'll show you," she answered.

A few minutes later, Mulder found himself in a small, white cinder-block room in the basement of the hospital staring at a yellow-and-black warning sign that read, BIOHAZARD—MEDICAL WASTE. A disposal unit that resembled a gigantic vat took up most of the space in the tiny room. Scully spoke while tying the back of a blue hospital apron.

"All hospitals operate some form of medical waste processing," she explained. She flipped a splatter shield down in front of her face and began pulling on shoulder-length rubber gloves. "This unit disposes of surgical remains: amputations, excised tumors. They're ground up, then heated with microwaves. The result is a sterile soot that's used as road fill."

Mulder crossed his arms in front of his chest and shifted uneasily from foot to foot.

"Then there's going to be nothing left to find in here," he suggested.

"It depends," said Scully, "on how often they process their waste. If we're in luck, only once every few days."

Scully unlatched the door of the disposal unit, which hissed as the airtight seal was broken. She swung open the heavy door, and shined a flashlight into the interior. The light revealed countless sealed plastic bags, each containing bloody body fragments of various sizes.

"We're in luck," Scully said.

Mulder didn't share the sentiment. He had no desire to look, but curiosity compelled him. He thought he saw a big toe and shuddered with revulsion.

"How sure are you about this, Scully? Because if you're not sure I don't see any reason to disturb all this stuff."

The sucking and squelching noises were making Mulder queasy.

"Be careful there," Mulder quipped.

Scully ignored him and strained to reach even deeper.

"I think you're going to have to help me out here," she announced. "Your arms are longer."

Mulder opened his mouth to protest. But he changed his mind when Scully lowered her glare on him.

Within minutes, Mulder was decked out in appropriate biohazard gear. Reluctantly, he moved to stand next to Scully in front of the open disposal unit. He reached in gingerly and began feeling around. The search carried on in silence for several minutes before Mulder spoke, wincing.

"I think I got the toy surprise."

He groaned as he struggled to bring the object up from the bottom of the chamber. Once he'd gotten it to the top, Scully shined her flashlight on it.

"Leonard Betts," Scully confirmed, recognizing the face from the file folder.

"His head, at least," Mulder declared, "but where's his body?"

Mulder set the head down and both he and Scully felt around in the bin some more, plunging deeply into the vat of flesh.

"It's not down here, Scully," Mulder stated, withdrawing his arms. "There's not enough room."

Scully continued the search as Mulder shucked off his gloves and posed a question.

"What if he didn't dispose of the body, Scully? What if, somehow, he got it out of here?"

"Then why take time to dispose of the head?"

Mulder considered this as he untied his lab apron.

"Maybe there's an answer there," he said, gesturing toward the severed head perched atop a mound of body parts. "Something you can check out."

Scully continued to methodically inspect the disposal bin as she spoke to Mulder.

"We already know how he died: an automobile accident. What more is there to know?"

"Maybe nothing," Mulder pondered. "But it's about all we have to go on at the moment. Why don't you see if there's someplace you can examine Leonard Betts's head."

Scully glanced over to her partner, aware of how anxious he was to get out of this room.

"While you do what?" she asked.

"Check out Betts's house. We know how he died, I want to see where he lives."

"Lived," Scully emphasized.

"Lived," Mulder repeated.

Chapter Three

The digital readout on the laboratory scales flickered through a series of numbers before settling on a weight. Scully, dressed in scrubs and working alone, lifted Leonard Betts's head out of the tray and set it down on the autopsy table. She clicked on her tape recorder and began dictating. The microphone picked up both Scully's voice and the dull scraping of steel on steel as she arranged her instruments on the table.

"Case number 2268–97, Leonard Betts," Scully said unemotionally. "As the remains are incomplete, all observations refer to a decapitated head. Weight: ten pounds, nine ounces."

Scully began a visual examination of the head, rotating it with her gloved fingers.

"The remains show no signs of rigor mortis or fixed lividity." Scully pulled open the eyelids. "Nor do the corneas appear clouded. This would seem inconsistent with the witnessed time of death, now"—Scully referred to a clock on the laboratory wall—"nineteen hours ago."

Scully pondered the phenomenon. She'd read of cases in which the bodies of the deceased remained remarkably preserved for days after their deaths, but those had been under specific climatic conditions or in cases of mummification. There was no way this head should look this . . . Scully struggled for an adjective, then settled on *good*. She picked up a scalpel and dictated.

"I'll begin with the intermastoid incision."

Scully placed the tip of the scalpel behind Leonard Betts's right ear and prepared to draw it over the top of the scalp. As she forced the blade down on the cold skin, Leonard Betts's eyes flew open.

"Oh, God." She gasped.

Scully jumped back, sucking in air and dropping the scalpel, which pinged against a drain in the floor. She put her hand to her chest and breathed deeply to stop her heart from racing. Scully stared at the head on the table in front of her. It stared back, wide-eyed and motionless.

Nothing.

Scully knew she hadn't imagined it. Betts's eyes remained fixed on her. As she took a step forward, working up the nerve to continue the autopsy, Betts's mouth opened. At first the movement was almost imperceptible. Then the mouth closed again.

Trembling, Scully watched as Leonard Betts's eyes slowly closed.

The manager of the small complex where Leonard Betts had lived instructed Agent Mulder to follow him up a flight of stairs. He told Mulder the same thing he'd told the police officer he'd spoken with on the phone: that Betts was quiet, paid his rent on time, and that he wished he had more tenants like him.

Mulder spotted the door on the second story with a shiny metal D tacked up on it.

"This one here?" he asked.

The manager responded with a grunt and pulled a key out of a retractable ring clipped to his belt.

The muffled sounds of men talking followed by the rattle of a key in the lock were clearly audible to the figure who hid in the shadows of the darkened apartment. Before the door opened, it sprinted quietly from the living room toward the bathroom.

A moment later, Agent Mulder was inside the apartment, relieved that the manager didn't insist on accompanying him.

"Thanks," he said to the older man, who nodded and headed back toward the staircase.

Mulder flipped on the light and shut the door before glancing around. There was nothing stylish about Leonard Betts's small apartment. His furniture—a bed, table, and three chairs—was the sort of mismatched collection typically acquired at garage sales or secondhand stores for ten bucks an item. *Spartan* would have been a generous description of the decor were it not for the rows of bookshelves that lined one complete wall of the apartment. The books themselves were hardcover medical texts, for the most part. Mulder ran his fingers over a few of their spines before drifting out of the living-room area and into the kitchen. Resting on the counter that separated the two rooms was a small, framed newspaper article. Mulder picked it up. The headline read, BETTS NAMED EMT OF THE YEAR. The story included a photo of a somber Leonard Betts dressed in a coat and tie. Setting it back down, Mulder passed through the kitchen on his way to the bathroom. He turned on the light, then stopped in his tracks.

The bathtub was filled with an opaque, reddish-brown fluid. At first Mulder thought it might be blood. Then he noticed that the liquid had splashed across the tile floor. In these smaller puddles, he could see that the liquid was thinner than blood, and slightly tea-colored. Mulder's eyes followed the trail of puddles. They led from the bathroom floor onto the toilet seat, then up to the ledge of an open window. A pile of stained clothes lay on the floor. He knew where he had seen them before.

Mulder stepped over toward the window. The gauze curtains had similar stains. He gazed out over the fenced yards of the residential neighborhood. He heard dogs barking, and wondered if he'd just missed whoever—or whatever—had left these tracks.

Mulder turned back around and squatted next to the bathtub for a closer look. Hesitantly, he dipped a finger into the liquid, rubbed it between his fingers, and sniffed. He thought he recognized the scent. He reached over and opened the cabinets below the sink.

Inside he found several one-quart bottles of povidone-iodine antiseptic solution.

As Mulder paused to consider why there was a bathtub full of iodine solution, his cell phone rang.

"Hello," he answered distractedly, glancing back through the open window.

On the other end, Scully paced the width of the Monongahela Pathology Lab.

"It's me," she said, as soon as Mulder answered. "I've run into kind of a unique situation here."

"What'd you find?" Mulder asked.

"Uh, so far, not much," Scully told him. "I've run a PET scan on Leonard Betts's remains—four times now. Each time, the image comes out degraded. Like it's fogged."

"Just like the security footage," Mulder noted.

"Yeah, but this is cutting-edge technology, and the technicians say the machine is working perfectly." Scully frowned. The results were frustrating her. "They say the only thing that would account for the image distortion would be some form of radiation, though I can't see how or where it would be emanating from."

Scully waited for Mulder to respond. She knew he was trying to digest this new information.

"What'd your examination uncover?" he asked finally.

Scully dropped her eyes to the ground. She was glad Mulder wasn't there to see her look of embarrassment.

"I, uh, haven't actually performed one yet."

"Why not?" Mulder asked her, curious, not angry.

Scully shifted uneasily and checked to make sure none of the lab technicians were within earshot.

"I've encountered—" Scully forced herself to take a breath and start over. "I've encountered an extremely unusual degree of postmortem galvanic response."

"The head moved," Mulder said, translating instantly. Scully didn't know whether she was grateful or annoyed that he didn't sound surprised.

"It"—Scully shook her head. She couldn't believe these words were coming out of her mouth—"blinked at me."

She quickly tacked on a disclaimer as she resumed pacing. "I mean, it's just galvanic response—residual electrical activity stored chemically in the dead cells."

"Blinked or winked?" Mulder cut in.

Scully pictured the sly grin on her partner's face.

"You're afraid to cut into it," he said. She frowned, a bit annoyed, as Mulder continued his needling. "You're not saying it's alive, are you, Scully?"

Scully exhaled loudly into her cell phone. "No, Mulder. I'm certainly not saying that at all."

"Has it crossed your mind that maybe it's not quite dead, either?"

"What do you mean, Mulder?"

"I'm standing in Leonard Betts's apartment. The clothes worn by the person in those video grabs are here on the floor, Scully. And it looks like whoever was wearing them made himself right at home."

Mulder surveyed the living room then moved back toward the bathroom before concluding, "Maybe he was home."

Scully stared deadpan into space.

"Leonard Betts?" she asked. "Without his head?"

A thousand punchlines flew to her mind, but Scully had the disconcerting suspicion that her partner was serious. "Mulder, I don't even know how to respond to that."

Mulder shrugged. He knew how it sounded. "Just in case," he told her, "I'm going to ask the local police to place the building under surveillance. Whoever was here might come back. I'll be in touch."

Mulder turned off his cell phone, stuffed it into his pocket, and exited the apartment.

Moments later, a bubble surfaced in the tub. Then two bubbles. Then three. Something stirring below the iodine solution sent liquid rushing in all directions. Then, slowly, a fish-belly white head broke the surface, and the face of a man silently poked half into view—the face of Leonard Betts.

But there was something wrong with the features. The ears lay flat against the head, and the nose barely jutted out from the rest of the face. Waxy skin ran all the way up to the mouth, which was completely devoid of lips. There were no eyebrows. The eyes themselves were tiny, and as the eyelids fluttered open the pupils Ping-Ponged back and forth, taking in their surroundings, alert and aware.

Chapter Four

Michele Wilkes was given two weeks of sick leave to recuperate from her crash injuries. She took one day, sat home brooding, then called in and said she'd be back the following morning. Her face was still purple around the eyes and across her right cheekbone. A butterfly bandage covered the wound on her forehead.

She refilled a plastic coffee cup in the hospital's break room and exited through the emergency-room double doors. On her way to the ambulance, she heard someone call her name.

"Michele?"

The sound startled Wilkes. She was still a bit jumpy. A handsome man in a long dark trenchcoat approached her. He flipped open his wallet to show her his badge.

"Michele Wilkes?" he inquired.

"Yes?" Wilkes replied, glancing down at the photo identification.

"I'm Agent Fox Mulder with the FBI. You were Leonard Betts's partner?" Mulder could tell from the woman's expression that her emotions were running close to the surface. He adopted a softer tone of voice.

"They told me you were coming back to work today."

Wilkes nodded and managed a weak smile.

"Yeah. Figured I should get back on that horse," she said.

Mulder returned the smile. He knew this wasn't going to be easy for her, but she had information he desperately needed.

"You're on record as the person responsible for the disposition of Leonard Betts's remains."

Wilkes nodded. "He didn't have any family—no friends either, as far as I could tell."

"Aside from you?" Mulder interjected.

Wilkes thought about the question for a moment. The answer she came up with saddened her. "I liked him, but I wasn't really his friend. He didn't let people get that close."

"I'm not sure I could even call myself his partner," she told Mulder. "Mostly I just tried to stay out of his way."

The comment struck Mulder as odd—not necessarily the words, but the uneasiness with which she said them.

"Why's that?"

"He didn't need me," she said without resentment. "He didn't really need anyone. Leonard was the most amazing medical technician. He could diagnose illness better than any doctor I've ever seen. You know how they say some people can tell what's wrong just by looking at you?"

"Mmm-hmm." Mulder nodded.

"Leonard could do that. Especially with cancer. I always told him he should have been an oncologist or something. He even volunteered weekends in the cancer ward. Read to the patients, stuff like that."

The news piqued Mulder's curiosity. He filed it away mentally and continued his questioning.

"Was there anything else about him? Anything odd?"

"No," Wilkes replied, shaking her head. She thought harder, then added, "He never got sick. That was always pretty amazing. Doing what we do, you know. He was the picture of health."

"Was he ever injured on the job?" Mulder asked.

"No. Never. I mean, until . . ." Wilkes's voice evaporated. Mulder hurried to fill in the gap.

"Yes, I know," he said, trying his best to sound understanding.

Wilkes looked at Mulder before proceeding.

"I'm sorry," she told him, "but I don't really see what all this has to do with someone stealing Leonard's body. I mean, it almost sounds like you're investigating Leonard."

Mulder casually chuckled. "No, no. Thanks for bearing with my questions," he assured her. "I appreciate your taking the time."

Mulder turned and headed off. Wilkes watched him walk away, wondering what that had been all about.

Back inside the hospital, Scully watched as Leonard Betts's severed head emerged from a drum-sized steel vat full of thick, syrupy liquid. Steam rose out of the vat. An electric winch positioned over the tank whined as it continued to reel up the severed extremity. The head was now coated in something resembling clear plastic.

Scully had spent the entire morning in the Monongahela pathology lab setting up the procedure. She hadn't really expected Mulder to show up, but he arrived just as she and the hospital's pathologist—a humorless man—began the test. Now she and her partner were staring at the dripping head.

"This procedure is called biopolymerization," explained Scully. "It's basically a high-tech mummification process. Remains are dipped in an epoxy. Once it cures, the specimen can be sliced for examination."

"Or," Mulder noted, "you got yourself a nice paperweight."

Scully gave her partner a sidelong glance and sighed. "At any rate, I should have some autopsy answers for you soon."

Eventually, she and the pathologist produced the sample they were shooting for: a cross section of Leonard Betts's head, sliced as thin as a piece of paper. The pathologist held up the specimen pressed in a glass frame. To Mulder it looked disturbingly like a skull-shaped piece of luncheon meat.

"I'm starting with an anterior slice from your Mr. Betts," the pathologist remarked, "one favoring the frontal lobe."

As he spoke, the pathologist placed the giant slide beneath a large binocular microscope and peered into the eyepiece. He adjusted the focus, and his eyebrows furrowed in confusion.

"Well, this is certainly strange," he mumbled under his breath.

"What?" Scully asked.

"Is there something wrong with the image?" Mulder wanted to know.

"In a manner of speaking," the pathologist responded. "Here, see for yourself." He flipped on a video feed attached to the scope, bringing a video monitor to life. Mulder and Scully leaned closer as the image of the magnified specimen came into view. To Mulder it meant nothing. To Scully the image meant a good deal more.

"Oh my God," she said, amazed. "His entire brain looks like one giant glioma."

That was a word Mulder recognized. "He had cancer?" he asked.

"He was riddled with it," Scully responded. "Every cell in this sample, essentially every cell in his head and brain, all appear cancerous. It's completely pervasive."

That didn't make sense to Mulder. "Could someone live in this condition?"

"Live?" The pathologist snorted. "This condition isn't even possible in my experience. This man would have been long dead before reaching such an extreme metastatic stage."

"How, then, do you explain it?" Mulder asked, posing the question already on Scully's lips.

The pathologist shrugged. "Maybe the polymerization process distorted the sample somehow." He glanced back into the microscope. "Maybe we're not really seeing what we think we're seeing."

Mulder bit the tip of his thumb and stared at the video screen. "Or maybe," he speculated, "we're actually seeing it clearly for the first time."

"What are you suggesting?" Scully asked.

Mulder gave a slight grin and raised his eyebrows. He pointed at the giant slide. "That we get one of these slices to go."

Michele Wilkes signaled left and swung the ambulance onto the street leading to the hospital parking lot. It had been a busy day for EMTs, whose voices crackled back and forth with dispatchers for the entire trip. Wilkes listened as a driver she knew came over the speaker.

"Monongahela, one-thirty-six en route with male, age twenty. No visible injuries. Breathing stopped. Not responding to CPR. Please advise."

Wilkes couldn't help thinking that Leonard would have known what to do.

"Dispatch, somebody pick up please," came the plea.

She listened to the radio as she pulled the ambulance in front of the emergency room door. Her new partner sat in the back and tended to an elderly woman. Wilkes put the vehicle in park as the other EMT prepared the patient for unloading.

Just as she was taking the keys out of the ignition, a familiar voice issued forth from the speaker, stopping her in her tracks.

"Mobile two-oh-eight to base. Requesting patch with unit one-thirty-six."

Wilkes hesitated. She reached over and turned up the radio's volume.

It couldn't be.

The voice continued. "One-thirty-six, this is Allegheny Catholic two-oh-eight. I know you're up to your ass in alligators, but it sounds like your patient may be in anaphylactic shock."

Wilkes froze in disbelief. It was Leonard.

"Confirm this," she heard the voice—Leonard's voice—say, "and treat with point three milliliters epinephrine autoinjector."

The conversation continued with Ambulance 136 confirming Betts's diagnosis, then requesting a repeat of the recommended treatment.

"It can't be . . ." Wilkes whispered. "Leonard?"

"Hey, that seems to be working. Good call, two-oh-eight," Ambulance 136 responded. "Thanks for the tip."

"I'm glad I could help," Leonard's voice said.

Behind her in the ambulance, Wilkes's new partner was hauling the gurney out of the back of the vehicle. He noticed Wilkes sitting frozen in the driver's seat.

"Michele," he snapped, "let's go, here."

Wilkes pulled herself together enough to exit the vehicle, but she left the door open, listening intently to the haunting voice of her former partner. She wondered whether she was experiencing early symptoms of dementia.

Leonard could probably tell her.

Chapter Five

University of Maryland Professor Charles Burks was aware that some people thought he was crazy. Or at best they considered his studies to be some sort of pseudoscience. "Some people" included a number of his peers in the biology department, as well as most of the university administration. *Thank God for tenure*, he thought. Besides, he knew he hadn't gone off the deep end, and so did the FBI agent who'd brought him this tissue sample. His partner was another story. Burks could tell from her posture that she was—to put it mildly—a skeptic.

Burks turned off one set of light switches, plunging the lab into darkness. The switches he flipped on gave the room a red glow characteristic of darkrooms. Then he got to work. Although he was short and round, Burks possessed enough energy that Scully and

Mulder had to speed-walk around the darkened lab just to keep up with him. Burks couldn't help himself. He was excited. This sample was unlike any he'd worked with—a complete cross section of a human head. He placed the sample flat on a twenty-by-twenty-four-inch sheet of photographic paper.

"I've never worked with a sample of human tissue before," he told the FBI agents as he attached a grounding wire to the specimen with gloved hands. "What exactly are you looking to find?"

"I'll tell you if we find it," Mulder replied. He didn't want the experiment to bend to anyone's expectations.

Scully couldn't contain her curiosity any longer. "Are you ever asked to defend this as a legitimate scientific process, Dr. Burks?" she asked.

Burks was used to this kind of attitude. He no longer got defensive. Instead, he humored his detractors.

"Only if you're not happy with the results," he replied with a grin.

Mulder knew this wouldn't satisfy his partner. He rushed to the doctor's defense. "Chuck did some of the pioneering work in Kirlian photography here in the U.S.," he told Scully.

"Although I prefer the umbrella term *aura photography*," Burks added, powering up a set of machines that quietly began to hum. He turned to Scully and explained the process.

"Basically, by applying high-frequency electricity, I'm able to photograph an organism's coronal discharge."

It wasn't a term Scully was familiar with. "Coronal discharge?" she repeated.

Mulder jumped in. "The life force. What the Chinese call Chi. Its existence is an accepted fact in Eastern cultures."

"And the theoretical basis of holistic medicine, of acupuncture," Scully observed, choosing to ignore Mulder's superior tone. "But I don't see what application it has here."

"It may account for the fogging on your PET scan of Leonard Betts's head," Mulder suggested.

A red pilot light on the machine began to glow. Burks pressed a button and an induction coil crackled. Tiny streams of electricity sparked across the surface of the specimen. A pale halo, clearly visible, surrounded it for two or three seconds before fading. Burks grinned. This was a thrilling moment.

"With this equipment, I'm able to capture phantom

images of whole leaves that were cut in half." He beamed, removing the exposed photographic paper. He hurried across the lab and slid it into a tub of developer. "Or the vestigial image of a lizard's tail even after it's been cut off. Which, you have to admit, is pretty cool."

Burks spoke with more than a hint of pride as he agitated the print in its bath. Scully gave Mulder a wary glance as the doctor pulled the print out of the tray and held it up.

"I think we've got something here."

Mulder moved closer to look. Despite herself, Scully eased forward as well.

"I don't know if this is what you're looking for, but there's definitely some energy at work here."

Burks hung the translucent image on a lighted viewing board. He flipped on the switch and the fluorescent tubes flickered to life. The cross section of Betts's head was revealed in silhouette, the edges marked by a glowing fringe of electricity.

But the silhouette didn't end where the sample did. It continued down into a phantom neck and shoulders, which faded off the edge of the photograph. Mulder was the first to speak.

"Would you believe this man's head had been decapitated, Chuck?"

Dr. Burks assumed Mulder was kidding.

"Oh, come on." He chortled, before realizing Mulder was serious. "No way."

"Way," Mulder deadpanned.

Mulder turned back to his partner. "Are we happy with the results?"

Scully could only stare at Mulder and wonder what strange hypotheses were popping into his head.

Scully clutched the envelope containing Leonard Betts's tissue sample and the aura photograph supplied by Dr. Burks as she and Mulder left his office. She didn't have to wait long to find out what Mulder was thinking.

"I don't know about you," Mulder declared, "but those sure as hell looked like shoulders to me."

Scully shook her head. "I'm not sure how to explain that photo or even what it proves," she replied.

"What if it proves Leonard Betts is alive somehow?" Mulder suggested.

"Mulder!"

Mulder stopped and faced his partner. "You said

before that Betts's tissue was consumed by cancer," he began. "What are cancer cells but normal cells growing rapidly, out of control? Usually caused by damage to their DNA."

"I have no idea where you're going with this," Scully interjected.

"Just listen," Mulder continued. "What if there was a case where the cancer wasn't caused by damaged DNA? What if cancer was not an aggressive or destructive factor, but a normal state of being?"

Scully shook her head. She decided not to give Mulder a lengthy medical lecture on the impossibility of such a mutation.

"Even if that were possible, Mulder, he's been decapitated."

"Yeah, but what if the life force—his Chi or whatever you want to call it—somehow retained a blueprint of the man himself, guiding rapid growth not as cancer but as . . . regeneration?"

Scully stared at Mulder openmouthed. "You think Leonard Betts grew a new head?" she exclaimed, flabbergasted.

Mulder continued to expound upon his theory.

"The fluid I found in Betts's bathtub—it was povidone-iodine. It's often used by lab researchers on reptiles and amphibians to aid regeneration. We both know that salamanders have regenerated entirely new limbs, Scully."

She wasn't buying a word of what Mulder was saying.

"Salamanders are one thing," she pointed out. "But no mammal possesses that kind of regenerative power. And there isn't a creature walking the earth that can regrow its head."

"Some worms can," Mulder reminded her. "Cut one in half, you get two."

"Mulder, they're worms."

"I'm just saying it's not unheard of in nature."

Scully paused, putting Mulder's theory aside for the moment. There were more pressing issues. "Unheard of or not, someone is going to great lengths to dispose of the evidence."

Mulder could explain that as well. "Maybe he's just protecting his secret."

Before she could respond, Scully's cell phone rang. She answered it, without taking her eyes off Mulder.

"Scully," she said into the phone. Mulder watched as bleary-eyed graduate students exited a nearby classroom while he waited for Scully. "Great. Thanks," she said finally, punching the DISCONNECT button and pocketing the phone.

Mulder raised his eyebrows, hoping to get briefed.

"Well, Leonard Betts apparently did keep a few secrets. One of them being that he had an alter ego named Albert Tanner," Scully told him.

The name didn't register.

"Who?" Mulder asked.

"I had Danny run Betts's fingerprints. Two names came up. The first one was Leonard Betts. The second one was Albert Tanner. But unlike Leonard Betts, he has a living relative. His mother, Elaine Tanner. Interestingly, all three of them live—or lived—in Pittsburgh."

Mulder and Scully drove to the quiet residential neighborhood where their latest information said Elaine Tanner still resided. Rows of narrow, two-story wooden homes lined the streets. There were no lights on at the address Scully had been given, but Mulder insisted on going up to the door and knocking. Eventually, they saw a light flicker on through the tiny window in the door. A woman who appeared to be in her late fifties padded down the entryway and greeted them.

"Yes," she said to them, surprised at receiving strangers at the late hour.

Mulder took note of the woman's bright pink apron and her cheery disposition.

"Elaine Tanner?" Scully inquired. "I'm Agent Scully, and this is Agent Mulder. We're with the FBI."

The woman seemed to be caught off guard.

"Oh," she said. "What can I do for you?"

"Your son is Albert Tanner?"

The question appeared to confuse Mrs. Tanner, but after a pause she slowly nodded her head. Scully proceeded.

"May we ask you a few questions?"

Mrs. Tanner nodded again and opened the door wider. Scully and Mulder followed her into the parlor.

"You'll have to excuse me for one second," Mrs. Tanner told them, "I've got something on the stove."

The woman disappeared through a doorway in the back of the room. Mulder glanced down at a mahogany sideboard and noticed something.

"Scully," he remarked, pointing at a framed photograph propped up at one end.

Scully saw it, too—the photo was of the man they knew as Leonard Betts. Scully took the photo from

Mulder and held it closer to study it. Mrs. Tanner returned to the parlor smiling. Scully held the photo up to the woman.

"Ma'am, is this your son?" she asked.

Mrs. Tanner swelled with pride and her smile grew even wider. "Yes." She beamed. "That's Albert."

Scully hesitated, unsure of how to phrase her next questions.

"We know this man as Leonard Morris Betts," she began. "Are you familiar with that name?"

Mrs. Tanner's smile began to fade. "No," she answered.

Mulder attempted to expand the range of the question.

"Did your son travel under any aliases that you know of?" he asked.

"Why are you asking me about him?" Mrs. Tanner responded, her cheerfulness gone now.

There was a moment of silence as it dawned on the agents that Mrs. Tanner may have been uninformed with regard to her son's whereabouts. When Scully spoke again, she used her most delicate voice.

"Ma'am, are you aware that your son has recently died?"

Mrs. Tanner stared back at Scully as if she were crazy.

"What do you mean 'recently'?"

Scully and Mulder glanced at each other. "Mrs. Tanner, when did your son die?" Mulder asked her.

"Six years ago," she answered. She could tell that the agents weren't expecting this. "He was killed in an automobile accident. Why?"

"Mrs. Tanner," Scully asked in a level tone, "would it be possible for you to provide us with the death certificate? Some form of verification?"

"Of course," Mrs. Tanner replied, a hint of confusion in her voice.

As the woman moved away from them into an adjoining room, Scully stared after her. Mulder turned to his partner and raised his eyebrows.

"Confused yet, Scully?"

Chapter Six

Michele Wilkes's shift had ended two hours ago. She'd showered and changed into street clothes, then driven to Allegheny Catholic. The voice was still haunting her. The one from the radio.

"Up to your ass in alligators."

She'd heard only one person on the planet use that phrase—Leonard. And it was his voice, too, she'd swear to it. Tonight she would find Leonard Betts—or find out whether she was going off the deep end. Tentatively, Wilkes moved through the ambulance bay searching for Leonard. She noticed a couple of EMTs lounging in their unit waiting for a call. Wilkes approached the ambulance's passenger-side window.

"Excuse me," she said nervously, "I am . . . uh . . . I'm looking for an EMT. The man driving unit two-oh-eight?"

The EMTs glanced at each other. The black female riding shotgun spoke to her partner.

"The new guy?"

The driver nodded, and she turned back to Wilkes. "Yeah, two-oh-eight's over there. He just went off shift, but you might still catch him."

Wilkes thanked them and made her way toward Ambulance 208, parked a hundred feet away in the gloom between streetlights. As she moved closer, Wilkes noticed a lone man with an EMS case climbing out of the vehicle. Though it was impossible to make out his features, the shape of his body looked right, as did the walk. Wilkes's heart caught in her throat as she forced herself to call out.

"L-Leonard?"

The man glanced briefly in Wilkes's direction, then quickly but calmly walked away. Wilkes jogged after him, and when she reached the spot where she'd last seen him, she looked around. But she saw no one. Maybe she was losing it. She was ready to chalk the whole thing up to her mind playing tricks on her when she noticed something. An oak tree forty feet beyond the edge of the parking lot—the way the shadows from the streetlight fell, Wilkes could tell there was someone behind it.

Wilkes approached cautiously, taking an angle that allowed her to keep the shadow in sight without being seen. She stopped fifteen feet away, fighting the urge to turn and run. Then, reluctantly, the man stepped forward into the light.

It was Leonard Betts.

When Wilkes spoke, the words were barely audible. "Oh my God, Leonard. Is it really you?"

Betts gave her a faint, melancholy smile. Wilkes no longer felt scared—just stunned. She had to keep telling herself that this wasn't a dream, that Leonard wasn't really a ghost.

"Hey, Michele." Betts moved forward to hug his former partner, one arm stretched out for her. Wilkes backed up, unsure why she was becoming afraid. "It can't be you—how can it be?"

"It's okay," Betts assured her.

He took another step and reached around her, hugging her fully. She gingerly hugged him back, her head swimming. Part of her wanted to accept it without question. As Leonard held her, Wilkes could feel her pent-up guilt subside. He was alive; she hadn't killed him.

Betts swallowed hard. His eyes brimmed with tears. He could feel the fear in her giving way to joy. He didn't want to do this.

"It's okay," he repeated. "I just wish you hadn't found me."

"What are you talking about?" she whispered back to him.

Betts pulled a hand away from Wilkes's back. It held a large autoinjecting syringe.

"Leonard?" Wilkes looked at him, still hoping for an answer.

But Betts's only response was to press the hypodermic into a spot between her shoulder blades. The syringe pumped in its lethal concoction while Betts held his former partner tighter. It was only a few seconds before Wilkes began to convulse.

"I'm sorry," Betts whispered. "I'm so sorry."

Wilkes's body jerked against Betts's grip, but it was over within a moment. Her eyes rolled back into her head, and she went limp. Betts lowered Wilkes's body gently to the leaf-covered ground. He stared at her for a moment, wishing she'd never come looking for him.

"Hey, you there!"

Betts turned into the direct beam of a flashlight.

Shielding his eyes, he saw a burly security guard sprinting toward him from the direction of the hospital. Betts rose, vaulted over a railing, and sprinted down the sidewalk, away from his pursuer. The guard hesitated when he arrived at the point where he'd first spotted Betts. His flashlight beam illuminated Michele Wilkes's body. He stared for an instant into her unblinking eyes, then tore off after her attacker, who was still within sight.

"*Stop!*" he commanded. "*Stop where you are!*"

Betts ignored him and made his way to the parking lot, zigging between parked cars, eventually finding his beaten-up Dodge Dart. He searched frantically for his keys. He could hear the guard just seconds behind him. He found them! Betts inserted the key in the car door, but as soon as he turned it, he was blindsided by the diving security officer. Betts went sprawling against the pavement. Before he could recover, the guard was on top of him. The next thing Betts saw was the flashlight, raised high above his head, swinging down. The battery end bashed into his forehead. Betts clung to consciousness; it was his only hope. He managed to deflect the second blow with his forearm, but he didn't have enough strength to stop the powerful guard from slapping handcuffs on his wrist. Barely able to focus, Betts watched as the guard hooked the other ring onto the door handle of his own car.

"Stay there, you son of a bitch," he growled. The guard patted Betts down, but found nothing. He pulled the keys from the car door where they still dangled and pocketed them. Below him, Betts lay bleeding. Both men were breathing like heavyweight boxers. The guard pulled his walkie-talkie from his belt and clicked the TALK button.

"Ronnie, pick up, man!"

The guard stared back over to the grove of trees as he waited for the reply. A few moments later, a voice crackled through the walkie-talkie speaker.

"Go ahead."

"We got a situation in the employee parking lot. This guy attacked some woman. She's up in the ambulance parking area. Somebody get a doctor up there right away." The guard took one hard look at his prisoner before jogging up the sidewalk back toward the spot where he'd seen the woman's body.

Once the guard was out of sight, Betts rose unsteadily to his feet. He tested the handcuffs by jerking them hard against the door handle. Then he tried pulling on the door handle itself, to no avail. Casting a long, searching glance in the direction the guard had gone, Leonard Betts knew he didn't have much time before someone came to take him away. He needed to act now.

Using his free hand to grip the thumb of the hand that was in cuffs, he began to pull. Sweat beaded up on his forehead. His eyes squeezed shut. Betts gritted his teeth to keep from screaming. He tried to focus on the voices in the distance rather than on his own pain.

"Somebody get a stretcher."

"I can't find a pulse."

"I need to go check on that guy."

Then a sound closer to his ears—of his thumb popping out of its socket—followed by the sickening sounds of bone tearing loose from cartilage and flesh ripping apart.

Less than a hundred yards away, the security guard kneeled next to Michele Wilkes. Another guard and an ER doctor had arrived moments earlier. The guard could tell from the doctor's expression that the prognosis was grim. There was nothing more he could do there, so the guard headed back to the parking lot, silently wishing he had bashed the perpetrator a few more times with the flashlight. The creep deserved it.

As the guard approached the car, he slowed. He shined his flashlight on the spot where he had left Betts. He looked startled at first, then confused. The car was there. And the cuffs were there, too, dangling from the door handle. But the prisoner was gone.

The guard crept up to the car warily. As he turned into the gap between the Dart and the sports utility vehicle next to it he got a better look at the cuffs. On closer inspection he could see the fresh blood that dripped from them and splattered against the side of the door. The guard followed the trail of blood to the ground. What he saw first shocked, then nauseated him.

Resting on the pavement was Leonard Betts's thumb. It looked as though it had been torn off at the joint.

Chapter Seven

By dawn it was snowing. Small, wet flakes blew against Agent Mulder's face as he bent down in the Allegheny Catholic Hospital employee parking lot. Using latex gloves, he carefully picked up the severed thumb from the ground, examined it, and sealed it in a plastic evidence bag. Police radios chattered noisily in the background as uniformed cops cordoned off the area with yellow police tape. Hospital security guards patiently explained to exhausted employees coming off their night shift why they wouldn't be able to move their cars just yet.

Mulder followed the trail of blood on the ground to the handcuffs that remained attached to the door handle. He looked up in time to see Scully approaching from the area where Michele Wilkes's body had been discovered. He held up the evidence bag containing the thumb.

"Siskel or Ebert?" Mulder joked. Scully didn't laugh. "So what's the story?"

"Michele Wilkes was murdered, but if the security guard hadn't witnessed it, we might never have known that," Scully informed Mulder from beneath her umbrella.

"Why not?" Mulder asked.

"I found a spent autoinjector in the grass. She was given a lethal dose of potassium chloride," Scully explained. "Because it's an electrolyte found naturally in the body, coroners don't usually screen for it."

Mulder opened his umbrella as the snow began to fall harder.

"Betts was here, Scully. Wilkes must have discovered that. Then he killed her to protect his secret."

She nodded with growing apprehension. "The security guard ID'd him as her attacker. He was wearing an EMT uniform, but his coworkers say his name was Truelove."

"Scully, do you know how this man escaped?" Mulder showed her, gesturing toward the blood-spattered car door. "He tore off his own thumb. Because he knew he could grow a new one."

"Mulder, it just doesn't work that way," she insisted.

"But is it unimaginable?"

Scully gave Mulder a look that indicated she thought it was. But Mulder wasn't giving up.

"Maybe Betts's ability to regenerate is no greater a leap forward than our ancestors' ability to walk upright or communicate with language," Mulder suggested.

"Language . . . evolution—it's a process of steps, Mulder. Not leaps."

Mulder shook his head. "Recent evolutionary theory would disagree. What scientists call 'punctualism' or 'punctual equilibrium.' It theorizes that evolutionary advances are cataclysmic, not gradual. That evolution doesn't follow a straight line, but progresses in huge fits and starts. And that the unexplainable happens in the gaps—the gap between what we are and what Leonard Betts has become."

Scully gave Mulder's reasoning some degree of consideration. Then she spoke. "What you're suggesting is a man so radically evolved you couldn't even call him human."

Mulder shrugged, then smiled. "On the other hand, how evolved is a man who drives a Dodge Dart?"

Scully glanced at the car, not getting the joke. Mulder sighed and pulled another evidence bag out of his trenchcoat pocket. It contained the car keys the guard had taken from Betts. He jingled them in front of Scully.

Taking the keys from the bag, Mulder found the one for the trunk. He popped it open. The only thing it contained was a medium-sized ice chest. With Scully beside him, Mulder opened it. The chest was loaded with Ziploc bags full of tumors, the same kind he had seen in the bio disposal unit at Monongahela Hospital. The bags were soaking in melted ice. Scully uneasily picked up one or two of the bags and read the labels.

"Myeloid sarcoma. Epithelial carcinoma. These are cancerous tumors." Scully turned to her partner. "This is all surgical waste tagged for disposal. Why would he want this?"

Mulder had an idea, but it made him queasy even to consider it. "You may not want to know," he declared flatly.

The look of disgust on Scully's face told Mulder she might already be on the same page.

"Scully, there's a great possibility that Leonard Betts not only is cancer—"

Scully finished his thought. "—But that he needs

cancer to survive? You're saying this is . . ."

"Snack food," Mulder replied, verbalizing what they both had been thinking. "Wouldn't it make sense that evolution, natural selection, might incorporate cancer—the greatest health threat to our species—into our genetic makeup?"

What Mulder was suggesting ran counter to every respected theory on the subject.

"Why do I think Darwin is rolling over in his grave right now?"

"Ask yourself," Mulder said emphatically, "why is Betts an EMT? Why does he regularly visit cancer wards?"

Mulder nodded at the chest full of tumors. "Access."

As Scully considered this idea, a uniformed police officer clicked off his radio and approached her. He read to them from his notepad.

"Car's registered to one Elaine Tanner, 3108 Old Bank Road."

Mulder and Scully exchanged glances.

"You figure Mom knows her dead son's tooling around in her car?" Mulder asked sarcastically. Both agents knew the answer to the question.

The old woman had lied.

x x x

Elaine Tanner heard banging on the door, and although not completely unexpected, the number of police officers gathered on her front steps startled her. Regardless, she thought it best to meet them with a smile. The female FBI agent she had met two days before held up a piece of paper.

"Elaine Tanner, we have a warrant to search the premises."

The icy tone of the FBI agent was too much for Mrs. Tanner. Her pleasant expression began to darken.

Within minutes police officers were encamped in her parlor, searching through drawers and cabinets. Mulder told Scully he was going upstairs to look for something while she questioned Mrs. Tanner.

"Mrs. Tanner, we know your son is alive and that you're in contact with him. Tell us where we can find him."

Scully waited for a response, but the old woman wouldn't look her in the eye. Instead, she watched silently as one of the police officers pushed aside some of her favorite antique figurines.

"Last night, your son murdered a woman in cold

blood," Scully told her. "Lying to protect him makes you an accessory to that murder."

This time Scully got a reaction. Mrs. Tanner turned slowly around and looked at her. Just then, Mulder approached carrying a large bottle of povidone.

"Mrs. Tanner," he interrupted, "may I ask what you use this for?"

The old woman assumed an impassive expression. Mulder continued. "This is a pretty big bottle. You get a lot of cuts?"

Mrs. Tanner saw in Mulder's eyes that he had figured it out—he knew—some of it at least. If this were the case, she wanted them to understand. Understand and leave Leonard alone.

"When my son was eight years old," she slowly began, "there were two boys who picked on him because he was different. He just ignored them. He knew he was better than they were. One day they cornered him as he was walking home. They beat him up. He didn't even try to fight back. He just lay there taking the blows."

Mrs. Tanner turned, locking eyes with Scully. "So I don't believe you when you tell me he killed someone," she said. "But if he did, he had his reasons."

Scully spoke up. "What reasons, Mrs. Tanner?"

"God put him here for a purpose," the old woman said defiantly. "God means for him to stay—even if people don't understand. And that's all I've got to say."

Mulder and Scully both knew that they would get nothing more from her.

Chapter Eight

John Gillnitz didn't normally drink whiskey until the sun went down. Before dusk, he usually stuck to beer. Healthier that way. But Emily was driving him to the hard stuff. Emily was the reason John arrived at Club Tip Top. She was the reason for the seven shots of Jack Daniels he'd put away before the third quarter of the Steelers game.

John sat on his barstool, took one last drag on his Camel, and stubbed out the half-inch cigarette in an overflowing ashtray. He tapped the last one from the pack and had it lit before he'd exhaled all the smoke from the previous one. He crumpled the empty box and tried to shoot a basket into the trashcan across the bar. Nothing but floor.

John took another drag and hacked up a lungful of smoke. He signaled Steve for another shot. That always helped.

He looked around. It was nearly deserted. A couple of guys in a booth he'd just hustled in pool. He wanted to avoid them. And a thin, balding guy at the other end of the bar who'd been giving him the creeps all morning. First of all, the guy hadn't been drinking—well, club soda, but that didn't count. Second, John had caught Baldy staring at him more than once. He decided he'd best head home. He threw the twenty down on the bar, hoping it would cover his tab, then climbed down off his barstool.

Leonard Betts watched as the man with the long, scraggly beard weaved out of the bar. The way he was smoking and coughing, Betts would give the man another year—two at best. And they wouldn't be pleasant. Chemotherapy. Drugs. Surgery.

Betts got up and followed the bearded man. As he exited, the brightness of the afternoon momentarily blinded him. He'd been in the darkened bar for two solid hours, waiting for his thumb to regenerate. He spotted Gillnitz staggering toward his car—a beat-up red Camaro. Betts approached, keeping his healing hand tucked safely into his coat pocket. He glanced around until he was satisfied the lot was deserted. The drunken man struggled to get the key in the door of his car.

"Excuse me," he said quietly, getting the larger man's attention.

Gillnitz turned to face the stranger.

"I'm s-sorry," Betts stuttered. "You have something I need." Betts shook loose the disposable scalpel that he'd tucked into his left sleeve and let it fall into his good hand. As he lunged forward, the blade flashed in the sun. The attack was quick and vicious. Within seconds, it was over.

Chapter Nine

The search of Elaine Tanner's home had taken three hours, and, true to her word, Tanner had said nothing since revealing that God meant for her son to survive. The police were in the process of putting things back on the shelves. Mulder bounded down the stairs looking for his partner.

"Scully?"

Scully emerged from the parlor. "You found something?" she whispered. Mrs. Tanner was sitting within earshot, and Scully didn't want any information getting back to her son.

"No sign of him," Mulder whispered back. "Not so much as a stray sock. Except this."

Mulder handed Scully a receipt from U-Keep-It Storage.

"A storage locker?" Scully asked.

"There's a key on his key ring with the number one-twelve engraved on it."

Scully glanced across the room to Mrs. Tanner, who suddenly had begun staring at them with a keen interest.

"Let's check it out."

Through a seam in the closed storage building door a thin ray of light struck Leonard Betts from behind, creating a silhouette of his naked body. The faint glow around his head illuminated the blood spattered around his lips. His skin was wet with perspiration, his eyes bulging from their sockets.

Betts was out of his mind with pain.

He lowered his head and struggled with something inside him. It moved in his abdomen, tearing muscles, stretching his skin. The sound of bones cracking filled the small room. Then, whatever was passing through his chest climbed its way up to his neck. His throat ballooned. Betts threw back his head and opened his mouth shockingly wide, like a python swallowing a pig. But Betts wasn't attempting to swallow anything; he was giving birth—

giving birth to a new Leonard Betts.

As he screamed in agony, the bulge in his throat ripped its way out through torn flesh and the broken jaws of the old Leonard Betts's mouth. The old head fell away, useless. In its place was an unfinished replacement, pasty and featureless as the day he'd almost been caught in his own bathtub.

Mulder drove the rented sedan past a sign that read U-KEEP-IT STORAGE and entered the storage facility lot, a compound of cinder-block buildings with roll-up metal doors. He cruised up and down the rows until he found the garage-sized unit with the number 112 stenciled above the door. Mulder parked, and the partners got out of the car and approached the locked handle.

Just as Mulder pulled the key out of his pocket, he noticed something.

"Scully!"

She saw it, too. Blood, oozing out from beneath the crack of the door. Scully drew her pistol and took a position along the opposite side of the storage unit. Mulder unholstered his gun as well, bent down, and silently unlocked the door. He felt some resistance as he pulled up. Once he had it open about three feet, a dead body flopped backward into view. The man appeared to be in his late forties, with a long, graying beard. Scully was about to examine the gaping wound in the man's chest when she heard a car engine turning over inside the unit.

Mulder gave Scully a quick look, then yanked the door all the way open. Light streamed in across the garage floor covered in empty plastic baggies, Styrofoam coolers, and organ transplant boxes. A car idled a few feet back in the deep storage unit, and for the first time Mulder and Scully got a look at Leonard Betts alive, behind the wheel. Staring hard at the two agents, Betts revved the Camaro's engine, then popped the clutch and accelerated right at them. The tires squealed against the concrete floor. Mulder leaped toward Scully and pulled her out of the car's way as it ran over the lifeless, bearded corpse.

As the car cleared the building, Betts turned hard to the right and barreled toward the storage compound exit. Scully and Mulder scrambled to their feet. Mulder aimed his pistol and squeezed off a shot that blew out the back window of the car thirty yards away.

Scully's bullet ruptured the gas tank. The explosion was instantaneous, lifting the Camaro several feet off the ground before dropping back down—a rolling, fiery coffin for Leonard Betts.

Chapter Ten

The body of John Gillnitz lay under the cold light of an autopsy lamp in the Monongahela Medical Center morgue. The room was deserted except for the two FBI agents. Scully, dressed in autopsy scrubs, leaned over the body as she reported her findings to Mulder. She was troubled by what she had uncovered during the examination.

"Mr. John Gillnitz," Scully began. "Dead from massive blood loss due to what appears to be a very skillful removal of his left lung."

"Betts," Mulder declared forcefully.

"Doing what?" Scully shot back.

"Guaranteed, Scully—this man's medical records will show he had lung cancer, and Leonard Betts was in need of what he had."

Scully's brows furrowed. "How would Betts have even known that?"

"His partner told me he had an exceptional ability to diagnose cancer," Mulder ventured. "Maybe his need provided a kind of heightened sense."

Scully shook her head. "So he killed this man in cold blood. To what? Feed his hunger?"

"Not hunger," Mulder countered. "Betts was after sustenance. And his search may have become even more desperate as his regeneration created a greater need."

Scully sighed. She was tired of arguing theories. She glanced at Betts's charred corpse lying next to Gillnitz's. Like the bodies of others she had seen who had died in fires, Betts's arms were raised in front of his chest and his fists curled up as if the victim had spent his final moments boxing the flames. The body itself was a mass of red lesions and blackened skin, bits of which stuck to the autopsy table each time they were forced to move him. All of his hair had been burnt off, yet Scully couldn't help thinking that his head—and his face in particular—were remarkably intact.

"Well," she concluded, "whatever he was doing, Betts is taking his secret to his grave."

"Yeah, for the second time," Mulder pointed out. Scully frowned. Mulder's tone indicated that this might not be over.

"Mulder, Leonard Betts is dead. Of that I am absolutely certain. And he's not coming back."

"You would have said the same thing about Albert Tanner," Mulder contended.

"I don't understand."

"Six years ago, Albert Tanner was killed in a car accident, buried by his mother. Several days ago, the same man turns up as Leonard Betts. Explain that to me."

"Obviously someone is lying," Scully told him, frustrated, but not raising her voice. "Or the first death was staged."

"You want to bet on that?"

It had taken two days but Mulder had gotten the body of Albert Tanner exhumed. Now he and Scully were at the morgue at Monongahela Medical Center where the casket had been brought. The more recent remains of Leonard Betts were on an autopsy table next to the casket. The assistant used a metal crank to lift the lid off Albert Tanner's coffin, then moved out of the way for them. Scully covered her nose and stepped in for a closer look.

The body inside the coffin, incinerated six years earlier in a car accident, was frozen in the same pugilistic stance as Leonard Betts—but the similarities didn't end there. Though also blackened by fire and slightly mummified, the face clearly belonged to the same man. Mulder felt a degree of satisfaction from the surprised look on Scully's face.

Mulder and Scully swiveled their heads back and forth between the two bodies noting the remarkable similarities.

"Will the real Leonard Betts please stand up?" Mulder asked, somewhat jovially.

But Scully wasn't convinced that easily. "Mulder, these two men may be no more than monozygotic twins."

Mulder looked at her seriously. He'd done a lot of thinking in the past three days. "I don't think so, Scully. I think what we're standing witness to here goes far beyond the regeneration of a thumb or a limb, or even a new head."

"Mulder, I don't know what you're getting at here.

Regeneration of an entire body? I don't know why I'm standing here listening to this."

"Because," Mulder answered, "I think the fiery crash that killed this man was a ruse, a decoy, and that this man lying here is still at large."

Chapter Eleven

I'm scared, honey." Elaine Tanner squeezed the sponge she held in her hand, and a reddish-orange liquid poured out. She leaned over the bathtub filled with povidone-iodine and pressed the cool sponge to the lily-white skin of her only child.

"The FBI—they seem to know all about you," she continued.

She dipped the sponge back into the solution, this time squeezing the excess directly onto her son's back. He shivered but said nothing.

"They dug up the coffin. They found your . . ." Mrs. Tanner hesitated. She wasn't quite sure how to say it. ". . . friend," she said finally.

Mrs. Tanner was trying desperately to show her son how strong she could be. Part of her wanted to sob—for him, for herself—but she knew what she had to do.

If Leonard sensed she wasn't one-hundred percent sure about her decision, he would not perform the task necessary for his survival.

"I don't think they're ever going to leave you alone," Mrs. Tanner whispered. "I've seen police cars driving by the house, circling the block. I think they're watching us right now."

Leonard stirred in the cool liquid of the tub. He glanced down at his hands. His skin at this stage of regeneration was like Silly Putty stretched over his bones. Leonard listened to his mother. She was the only person on earth he knew he could trust.

"You're weak, Leonard. You have to restore your energy."

Mrs. Tanner waited a moment for that to sink in. "You know what you have to do," she told him.

Leonard didn't speak; he just shook his head. He didn't want to do what she was suggesting, didn't even want her saying the words. Then again, he thought, there was no other way. Mrs. Tanner forced herself to smile.

"You're here for a purpose, and you have to go on," she continued, running the sponge over her son's hairless scalp. He looked back up at her. His eyes were white, except for two pink irises. Even though his features—ears, nose, mouth—were still only crude precursors to what they would soon be, she saw the son she loved.

"I'm your mother," she told him, "and it's a mother's duty to provide."

Leonard Betts couldn't bear to look at his mother any longer. He turned away and in the metal spigot saw his own unformed reflection, wearing an expression of infinite sadness.

Agents Mulder and Scully sat in a rented sedan half a block down the street from Elaine Tanner's home. Mulder had offered to stake out the place by himself—he knew his partner thought it would be useless—but Scully had insisted on accompanying him.

So far, everything was quiet, apart from the noisy sound of crickets. Mulder kept his eyes on the house. He was certain that even if Leonard Betts was once again alive, he wouldn't just stroll through the front door, so Mulder focused on windows and shadows. He watched carefully as lights went on and off. He calculated the time in between, watching for anything that might indicate an extra person inside the house.

Scully took a sip of her coffee, then looked over at Mulder. "If this man exists, what makes you think he'd come back here?" she asked.

Mulder gave a shrug before answering. "He would assume he's a dead man in the eyes of the FBI," he explained, "and the only person connected to Betts, who knows his secret, is his mother. If we're going to find him again, it'll be through her."

Scully accepted his explanation for the stakeout. The silence of the night was interrupted by something that initially sounded far off, then increased steadily in volume: a siren.

Scully looked over to Mulder and saw that he, too, was confused about what this might mean. Suddenly, an Allegheny Catholic Hospital ambulance rocketed around a curve with siren blaring, its headlights momentarily blinding the two FBI agents. As the ambulance sped straight toward Elaine Tanner's home, its flashing lights sent red-and-white streaks bouncing crazily off windows of the old houses.

Mulder was out of the car first, with Scully right behind him. Both had their guns drawn, and they were sprinting. Ambulances meant Leonard Betts.

Mulder planted himself fifteen yards in front of the

vehicle before it came to a complete stop. He assumed a shooting position—legs shoulder-width apart, knees bent, both hands on his pistol. Although the lights from the ambulance prevented him from seeing any more than shadows within the cab, he aimed directly for the steering wheel.

"Get out of the truck!" he barked.

Scully flanked him at a slightly different angle. She could see two figures inside the cab.

"Hands up!" she commanded, also holding out her gun.

Whoever was inside the ambulance wasn't moving fast enough for Mulder.

"*Get out of the truck!*" he repeated.

The driver scrambled out first, and though Scully couldn't see much, she could tell he was bald and roughly the same size as Leonard. In any case, he was confused and frightened.

"Whoa, whoa," the man begged, his arms raised. "What the hell . . . ?"

The driver stepped toward Mulder. Scully gripped her pistol tighter, prepared to drop the target at the first hostile move, but as he stepped into the beam of the headlights, Scully saw that it wasn't Betts. She relaxed slightly. She was able to discern that the EMT exiting from the passenger door was Latina and female.

"What are you doing here?" Scully demanded, without lowering her pistol.

"W-w-we got a call," the female EMT stammered, her palms held up to Scully. "An elderly woman suffering chest trauma, blood loss. Thirty-one-oh-eight Old Bank Road."

The EMT glanced nervously at her driver. She was afraid for her own life and for the woman's inside the house as well.

"That's all we know," the driver interjected.

Scully believed them. "Stay here," she ordered.

Scully didn't have to say a thing to Mulder. They both turned and raced up the sidewalk to the house, Mulder hopping over a small picket fence on the way, then taking the porch steps in one bound.

Mulder kicked open the front door of the darkened house and spun his way into the parlor, his gun leveled. Scully, with her gun drawn, watched his back. Mulder turned toward his partner when he saw that the room was empty. Though they said nothing, the lights of the ambulance illuminated the room enough that a strategy could be deployed with a few knowing glances. Mulder headed to the kitchen in the back, while Scully cautiously climbed the stairs.

Mulder pushed his way through a swinging door into Elaine Tanner's kitchen. He had the uneasy feeling that he was walking into a trap, but that vied with the news that there was a woman in the house in need of medical attention. He strained his ears as he stole across the creaky linoleum floor, but all he could hear were Scully's light footsteps on the floor above him.

Upstairs, Scully had a similar feeling—that each door she opened might be one that a killer was hiding behind. A killer, sure. But Leonard Betts—the man she had performed two autopsies on? Her brain told her it wasn't possible, but this was small comfort against the fear that rushed into her mind and body with an almost tangible force. Scully had pushed open the doors to the bathroom and bedroom; there was one left. She held her Smith & Wesson up to her right shoulder, twisted the door handle with her free left hand, and pushed.

Lying on the bed before her was the reason the ambulance had been summoned. Scully lowered her gun.

"Mulder," she yelled down the stairs. "Get the EMTs!"

Elaine Tanner was lying on top of her bedcovers, unconscious. A pressure bandage had been expertly applied to a wound high on her chest at her collarbone, though blood was beginning to seep through the dressing. Scully bent down over the old woman. She heard Mulder enter the room behind her just as she lifted back the bandage and grimaced.

"She's got an open wound," she declared. Scully looked back to her partner, who didn't appear the least surprised. "A surgical cut."

"Three guesses what was removed," Mulder replied sardonically.

The EMTs entered the room, and Scully stepped back to give them space. The implications of this apparent home surgery confirmed Mulder's wild theory—that Leonard Betts was out there, that he had done this.

"He did this to her," Mulder fumed, "then he called an ambulance."

"Judging by the response time, that would mean he may still be here," Scully concluded.

Mulder shifted into high gear, exiting the bedroom to continue the search through the house. Scully turned back to the bed where the EMTs were administering to Elaine Tanner. Scully wondered whether this had been done to her by her son, or whether this had been something Mrs. Tanner had done for him.

Chapter Twelve

Within five minutes, the EMTs were lifting the gurney carrying Elaine Tanner up and into the empty ambulance where Scully stood guard. After convincing the EMTs that she was a medical doctor, Scully checked most of Mrs. Tanner's vital signs. Mulder jogged up to where Scully was standing. His search had been quick and frantic.

"Betts is gone, Scully," he told her breathlessly. "He must have set out on foot."

Scully gestured toward Mrs. Tanner. "She's going to make it, Mulder," Scully said calmly. "She's not out of the woods yet, but she might be able to tell us where he went."

Mulder digested this information and formulated a plan.

"You stay with her, Scully." Mulder reached into his

jacket pocket and pulled out his cell phone. "I'll call in the local PD to cordon off the neighborhood."

"Okay," Scully nodded. She climbed into the back of the ambulance and joined the female EMT. Each grabbed one of the double doors and slammed it shut. The female EMT called for the driver to hit it, and the vehicle sped away from the curb. The siren came on just as Mulder reached the police dispatcher, and he had to cover his ear to hear himself speak.

"This is Agent Mulder with the FBI."

He waited for the acknowledgment from the dispatcher before continuing. "I've got an emergency situation in progress. I need all available units to Thirty-one-oh-eight Old Bank Road. I'm searching for a murder suspect."

The ambulance raced through the suburban streets of Pittsburgh as Scully and the EMT kept a close watch on Elaine Tanner's heart rate. Neither liked what they saw. At 4:20 A.M., the driver turned into the Allegheny Catholic Hospital emergency room entrance, parking in front of the only lighted area of the building. He hopped out of the cab, sprinted to the rear of the vehicle, and threw open the double doors. His partner already had unlocked the gurney's wheels and prepared the patient for transport. The pair eased Mrs. Tanner out of the ambulance, then rolled the patient carefully through the hospital entrance. Scully remained in the back of the ambulance admiring their efficiency as she pulled out her cell phone to report to Mulder. He answered on the first ring.

"Mulder, it's me," Scully said, her breath visible in the chilly northern night. "We've got Mrs. Tanner heading into the ER, but she took a downturn en route. They defibrillated her to get her heart beating, but there's no chance of getting anything coherent from her—not tonight. What about on your end?"

Mulder listened as he walked along Old Bank Road. Three police cruisers were parked along the street, their blue-and-white lights sweeping in giant circles across the block as uniformed officers bustled from door to door.

"We're going house to house here, Scully," Mulder informed her. "I don't know what else to do."

As Mulder spoke, Scully stepped down from the rear bumper of the ambulance, the phone pressed to her ear. She watched as a surgeon inside the hospital met the EMTs and took charge of the patient. Scully began to follow them in, but suddenly she felt something hit her head. She stopped, reached up, and touched a hand to her head.

"They're bringing a county chopper in," Mulder continued, "but until then, I'd say Betts stands a pretty good chance of getting away."

As he spoke, Scully examined her fingertips. They were wet.

And reddish-orange.

Inhaling forcefully, Scully spun and saw a thin rivulet of povidone-iodine run down from the top of the ambulance above her. As the stream reached the top of the double doors, it dripped slowly, one drop at a time, to the pavement below. Mulder's voice was still in her ear.

"If he was able to get a ride or steal a car, he may be gone for good, but he obviously worked this thing out pretty well. So, if there's anything you can get out of Mrs. Tanner tonight—anything at all—"

Scully's urgent whisper interrupted him. "Mulder, get down here!"

"What?"

"Get down here now!"

Mulder didn't ask again. He punched off his phone and sprinted for the rental car.

Back at the hospital, Scully pocketed her phone. She unholstered her pistol and stepped quietly back onto the rear bumper. Using the door handle as a foothold, she climbed cautiously to peer onto the roof of the vehicle, leading with her gun. As her head rose up over the top, her eyes took in the evidence before her. No one was up there, but puddles of povidone-iodine, along with two reddish-brown handprints, were clearly visible.

Just as Scully was about to climb down, someone grabbed her foot—the one that held all her weight—and yanked it from the door handle. Scully suddenly found herself flying backward toward the pavement, but she never hit the ground. Whoever grabbed her foot now latched onto her waist and threw her into the back of the ambulance. Scully bounced off an equipment locker, which flew open on impact. Gauze, hypodermics, and plastic alcohol bottles spilled out. Scully rolled over onto her back and brought her gun to bear on her attacker.

It was Leonard Betts.

Or at least some version of Betts. He was wearing an EMT uniform, but Scully could see his unformed face clearly: his features seemed to be covered by a hideous layer of mutant flesh. She hesitated an instant before firing—just long enough for Betts to knock the pistol from her with the back of his pasty white hand. Betts picked up the gun and tossed it out of the ambulance, then shoved her roughly toward the cab. Scully's head slid hard into the base of the driver's seat. Dazed, she looked up to see Betts slamming the rear doors behind him. She was trapped. She could smell the povidone that clung to his skin. Then Betts held something up. It took Scully a second to focus in the darkness of the ambulance, but as he twisted it into the light Scully recognized it—a scalpel. Betts paused momentarily and stared down at her. Then he spoke.

"I'm sorry," he said to Scully, "but you have something I need."

Scully looked into his eyes. She was taken aback by the words, by what they could possibly mean. She had the strange impression that he was being sincere—that he truly was sorry for what he was about to do. She didn't have long to think about it, though. Betts lunged at her, the scalpel aimed directly at her chest. Scully managed to block the blow, grabbing Betts's weapon arm with her left hand and warding off the blade with her right forearm. He pulled his arm back and tried to slice into her again, but Scully deflected the scalpel, this time with her left arm. She drew back her free hand and unleashed a roundhouse right to Betts's jaw that sent him reeling. As he staggered, Scully was able to kick him square in the chest, knocking him back farther. She scrambled to her feet as Betts again charged at her. This time Scully was ready for the attack. She unleashed a powerful kick, smashing her heel into Betts's armpit. He stumbled backward. Scully's second kick stuck him in the ribs on the opposite side. She knew from the crunching sound that she'd broken his ribs. The force of the blow knocked Betts against the back doors of the ambulance. His hand with the scalpel slammed into the window, shattering the glass.

Betts howled, turning to look at his lacerated arm. Scully saw her opportunity to finish him off. But as she moved in closer, Betts spun around unexpectedly and delivered a vicious backhand to the side of Scully's face that sent her flying. With blood dripping from a cut above her eye, Scully rolled as far away from Betts as the cramped quarters of the ambulance would allow. She turned and gaped as Betts pulled his arm through the broken window back inside the vehicle. Blood gushed from a dozen lacerations in his arm. Betts fell to his knees in pain holding his bloody arm, but Scully saw that he'd managed to keep ahold of the surgical scalpel. She scanned the shelves around her desperately for a weapon—another scalpel, a large-bore hypodermic, a bone saw, anything. What she found on the floor next to her would have been amusing if she hadn't been fighting for her life—it was hardly a weapon. She flipped on the small, boxy unit. The machine whistled, and Scully gave a silent prayer that it would charge in time.

Betts staggered against the storage shelves, and the items that hadn't been knocked to the ambulance floor earlier rained down. All at once Betts seemed to remember his mission. He lunged across the ambulance toward Scully, the blade of his scalpel aimed at her throat.

Scully was prepared. She caught the brunt of her attacker's weight on the soles of her feet, but she let him roll up closer until they were nearly face-to-face. As the scalpel sliced toward her throat, Scully lifted a pair of defibrillation paddles and jammed them against Betts's temples.

With a loud *ka-chunk*, three hundred joules of electricity exploded through Leonard Betts's skull, blasting him backward through the double doors of the ambulance. He landed like a rag doll on the pavement in front of the emergency room entrance.

Scully could hear the sound of approaching police sirens. She sat up and dropped the defibrillator paddles. Still breathing hard, she stared at Betts's motionless form. She didn't take her eyes off of him, even as two EMTs and a security guard ran out of the building and surrounded the body.

What was it he had said?

You have something I need.

Chapter Thirteen

Mulder found Scully sitting in the passenger seat of their rented sedan. He noted the faraway look in her eyes. Mulder had forced Scully to seek medical attention. The butterfly bandage would probably keep the cut on her forehead from leaving a scar. Scully looked up as he approached the car. Her question didn't need asking.

"They pronounced Betts ten minutes ago," Mulder affirmed.

"He's dead?" Scully asked, needing reassurance.

Mulder gave a curt nod. He wasn't quite sure how to answer the question. "As near as anyone can tell."

Mulder could see that the news was somehow a relief to Scully, which wasn't like her. She usually preferred her captives safely behind bars. Mulder decided to proceed with less gloomy information.

"His mother's alive, though. Mainly due to how carefully Betts dressed the wound. She'll pull through . . . at least for the present."

The pause that came before Mulder's final remark concerned Scully. It meant that Mrs. Tanner might not be around for long even if she did pull through. Scully thought she knew why.

"Cancer?" she asked.

Mulder nodded, then checked his notepad. "Metastic rhabdomyosarcoma, to be precise. She previously underwent treatment for it. She was given a clean bill of health three months ago."

Scully considered the information carefully, remembering what Mulder told her Michele Wilkes had said—Betts had an exceptional ability to diagnose cancer. Mulder had even suggested that his need had provided a heightened sense. At the time, Scully considered the theory far-fetched at best. Now she wasn't so sure. Too much had happened. Too much of what Mulder predicted had come true.

Mulder sensed that his partner was preoccupied. He assumed, incorrectly, that it was related to the taking of a life. “You did a good job, Scully,” he said, smiling supportively. “You should be proud.”

Scully looked up at Mulder almost as if she were seeing him for the first time. She appreciated his kindness, but couldn’t manage a smile in return. For a moment, she considered telling Mulder what Betts had said to her. She wondered if he could figure it out on his own. He had read the reports. Was he already asking himself the same questions that Scully was asking? Why had Betts attacked Scully with a scalpel? Why hadn’t he used the gun when he had the chance? What was the motive for attacking Scully in the first place? After all, he already had escaped the crime scene. What was the benefit? There was only one answer in Scully’s mind, and it scared her to death.

When she finally responded, Scully hoped she merely sounded tired.

“Mulder,” she said in a shaky voice. “I want to go home.”

Mulder nodded, telling himself not to press. She would talk about whatever was bothering her when she was ready. He closed the passenger door of the rental car gently, then moved around the vehicle and settled in behind the wheel. As they pulled out of the parking lot, Scully watched the hospital disappear in the rearview mirror.

Back at her apartment Scully spent time writing up the report on Leonard Betts. When finished, she stared at the case long and hard, wondering exactly why she'd chosen to leave out the words Betts had spoken to her in the back of the ambulance.

They meant nothing.

She kept telling herself that all the way home.

Scully was ready for bed by the time the local D.C. television news show was over.

When Scully awoke, the red lights of the digital clock read 2:08. She lay in bed for a few minutes, then her body shook with a series of coughs. She rolled over for what seemed like the hundredth time that night and clicked on a bedside lamp. Maybe she would be better off reading. As her eyes adjusted, Scully noticed something on her pillow.

Drops of blood.

Scully reached out her hand and touched her pillowcase, then stared at the fresh blood on her finger. As she bent her head down, Scully felt a warm sensation on her lips. She touched her lip and felt the thin stream of blood trickling down from her nostril.

Dana Scully didn't need to consult any of the scores of medical texts stacked on shelves around her apartment. She recognized the symptoms. They were the warning signs of cancer.

THE X FILES™

Goblins

A novel by Charles Grant
Based on the television series created by Chris Carter.

Opening the X-Files ...
Meet Mulder and Scully, FBI. The agency maverick and the female agent assigned to keep him in line.
Their job: investigate the eeriest unsolved mysteries in modern America, from pyro-psychics to death row demonics, from rampaging Sasquatches to alien invasions.
The cases the Bureau want handled quietly, but quickly, before the public finds out what's *really* out there. And panics.
The cases filed under 'X'.

'*The X-Files* is a true masterpiece. There's no more challenging series on television and, as a bonus, it's also brainy fun.' *Los Angeles Times*

ISBN 0 00 648204 X

THE X FILES™

Whirlwind

A novel by Charles Grant based on the characters created by Chris Carter.

Unnatural disasters ...
Serial killers come in all shapes and sizes. But this one is particularly puzzling. There's no pattern to the mutilated bodies that have been showing up in Phoenix: both sexes, all races, ages, ethnic groups. There is no evidence of rape or ritual. Only one thing connects the victims, the natural disaster that killed them. One of the most unnatural natural disasters imaginable, leading to a most painful, most certain and most hideous death ...

'The series remains one of the most slickly produced hours on television, notable for its cryptic endings, and sharp, intelligent writing' *Variety*

'The most provocative series on TV' *Entertainment Weekly*

0 00 648205 8

THE X FILES™

Ruins

A novel by Kevin J. Anderson
Based on the television series created by Chris Carter.

LOST CITY, FOUND
When a well-connected American archaeologist, Cassandra Rubicon, disappears while exploring the lost Mayan city of Xitaclan, the incident becomes a case for FBI agents Mulder and Scully. They are investigators assigned to the X-Files, the strange and inexplicable cases the FBI wants to keep hidden – cases involving the paranormal, the supernatural, and possibly, the extraterrestrial.

Mulder thinks there may be more to this case than simply a missing team of scientists – namely ancient curses, blood sacrifices and deadly reptilian monsters lost in the jungle since before history.

Scully is, as always, more sceptical and likely to provide the logical explanations for her partner's unorthodox speculations. Meanwhile, a covert U.S. military commando team has been sent to investigate, and destroy, a strange electronic signal received from beneath the ruins – a signal aimed upward, at the stars ...

0 00 648253 8

THE X FILES™

Antibodies

A novel by Kevin J. Anderson
Based on the television series created by Chris Carter.

When a disease-ravaged body is found in the smouldering ruins of the DyMar genetic research lab, FBI agents Fox Mulder and Dana Scully fear that a deadly man-made plague is on the loose. As the agents investigating the X-Files – cases that the bureau deem unsolvable – Mulder and Scully must pursue the truth wherever it leads, even into the labyrinthine corridors of the FBI ... and beyond.

Racing to contain the lethal virus before it can spread, Mulder and Scully make a chilling discovery about the lab's most recent project: a promising but highly-dangerous bio-machine that can cure any disease and heal any wound, potentially even a doorway to immortality. But when a second corpse turns up, savagely mutilated from within, it's anything but theoretical. Could machines created to cure have learned to kill? As sinister forces close in, Scully fights to save the life of an innocent boy while Mulder comes face-to-face with a crazed and desperate man whose slightest touch brings agonizing death – and perhaps a resurrection more horrible still.

0 00 648252 X